Medieval Medical Care

Carmel Reilly

Medieval Medical Care

Text: Carmel Reilly
Editor: Rochelle Ransom
Design: Jennifer Warwick
Series design: James Lowe
Photo researcher: Corrina Tauschke
Production controllers: Renee Cusmano and Lisa Porter
Reprint: Siew Han Ong

Acknowledgements
The author and publisher would like to acknowledge permission to reproduce material from the following sources:
Bridgeman: pp. 4, 5, 6, 7, 15, 16–17, back cover; Corbis/Bettmann: pp. 1, 20, cover; Corbis/Cynthia Hart Designer: p. 14 (bottom right); Corbis/The Gallery Collection: p. 18; Corbis/Patrick Ward: p. 19; Corbis/Stapleton Collection: p. 13; Getty Images: p. 8;
Mary Evans Picture Library: pp. 3, 10, 12, 14 (left), 21, 22–23; Photolibrary: p. 6; Photolibrary/Cordelia Molloy: p. 11; Photolibrary/Gabriele Meermann: p. 14 (top right); Photolibrary/L Newman & A Flowers: p. 16;
Richard Morden © Cengage Learning Australia: p. 9.

Every effort has been made to trace and acknowledge copyright. However, if any infringement has occurred the publishers tender their apologies and invite the copyright holders to contact them.

Fast Forward Independent Texts
Level 18

For product information and technology assistance,
in Australia call 1300 790 853;
in New Zealand call 0508 635 766

For permission to use material from this text or product,
please email **aust.permissions@cengage.com**

ISBN 978 0 17 017985 0
ISBN 978 0 17 017898 3 (set)

Cengage Learning Australia
Level 7, 80 Dorcas Street
South Melbourne, Victoria Australia 3205

Cengage Learning New Zealand
Unit 4B Rosedale Office Park
331 Rosedale Road, Albany, North Shore NZ 0632

For learning solutions, visit **cengage.com.au**

Printed in Australia by Ligare Pty Ltd
2 3 4 5 25 24 23 22 21

Medieval Medical Care

Carmel Reilly

Contents

CHAPTER 1

A HARD LIFE

The Middle Ages in Europe
began just after the fall of the Roman Empire
in about 450 AD, and ended around 1450 AD.

Life in the Middle Ages was much harder
than it is today.
Although some people were quite well off,
others had to work very hard
for very little money.

Many people lived in very basic houses
and without much food.
Staying healthy was not easy.

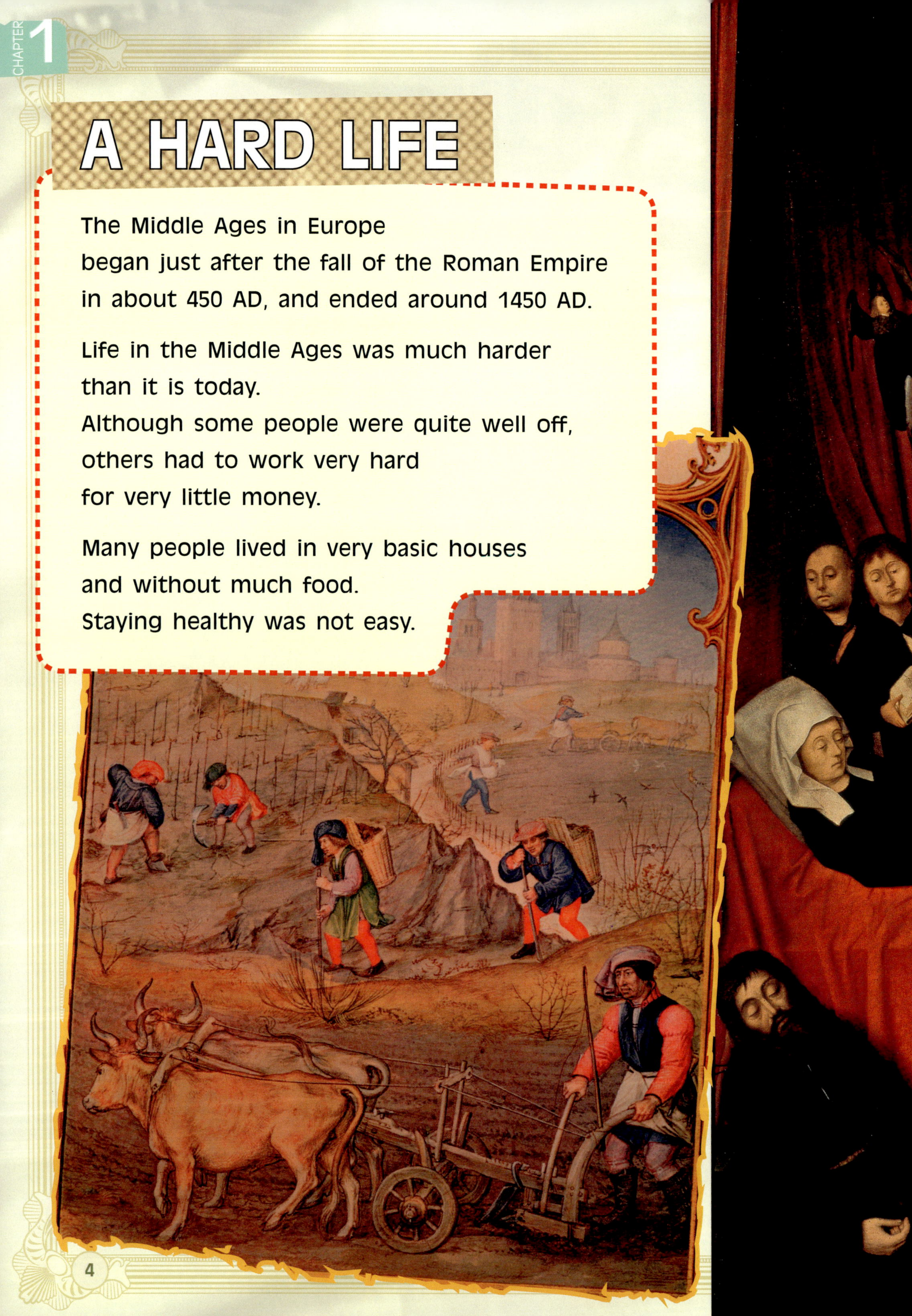

Sickness was common
and when people became seriously ill,
they usually died.

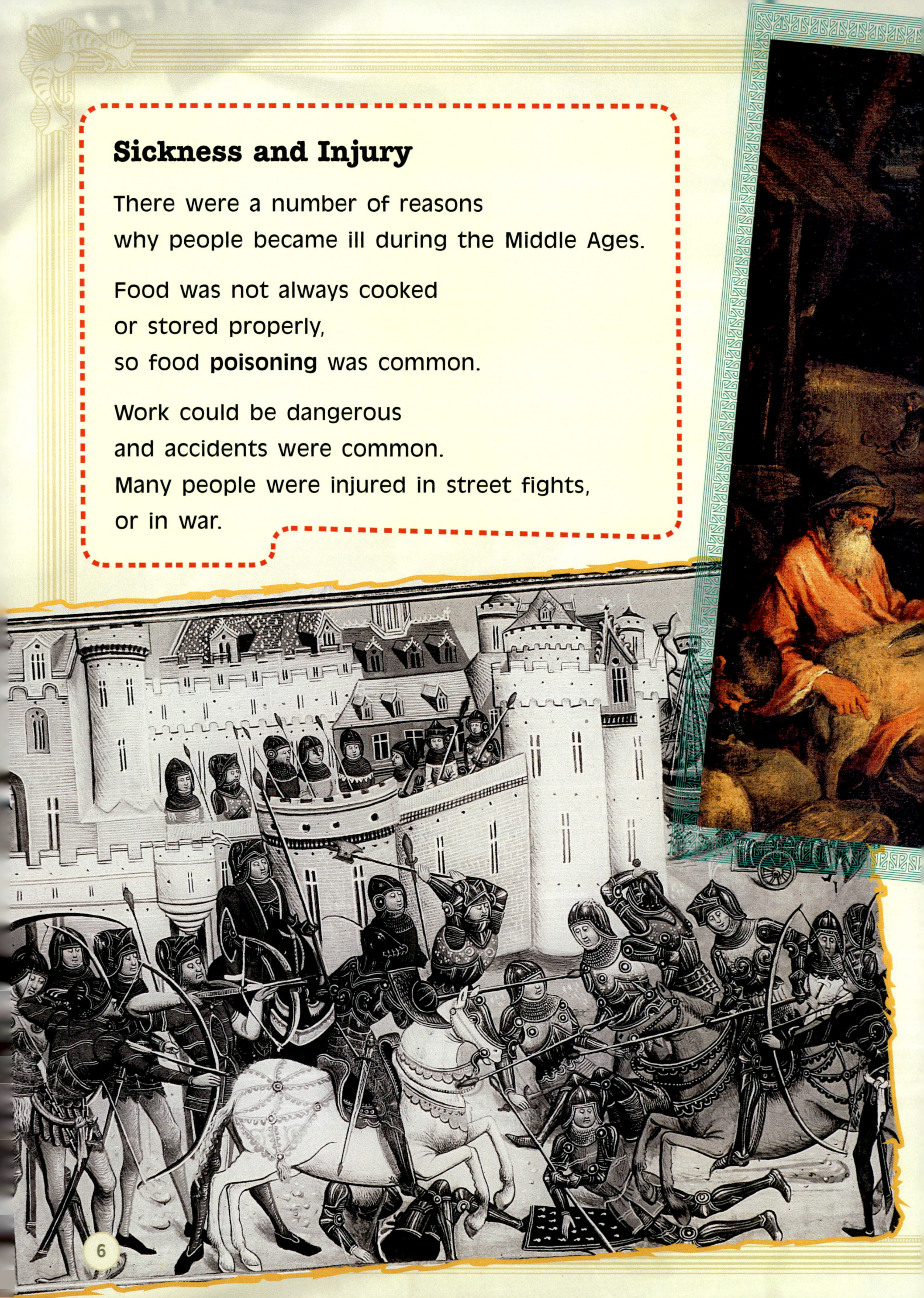

Sickness and Injury

There were a number of reasons why people became ill during the Middle Ages.

Food was not always cooked or stored properly, so food **poisoning** was common.

Work could be dangerous and accidents were common. Many people were injured in street fights, or in war.

People who worked closely with animals often caught diseases.
They also caught diseases from dirty water.
These diseases were then passed onto others because people didn't wash their hands or keep things clean.

CHAPTER 2

IDEAS ABOUT ILLNESS

Balance

In the Middle Ages, people in Europe thought that the world was made up of four different forces – earth, water, fire and air.

They also believed that the human body was made up of these same forces. It was believed that when the four forces were out of balance in someone's body, the person would become ill.

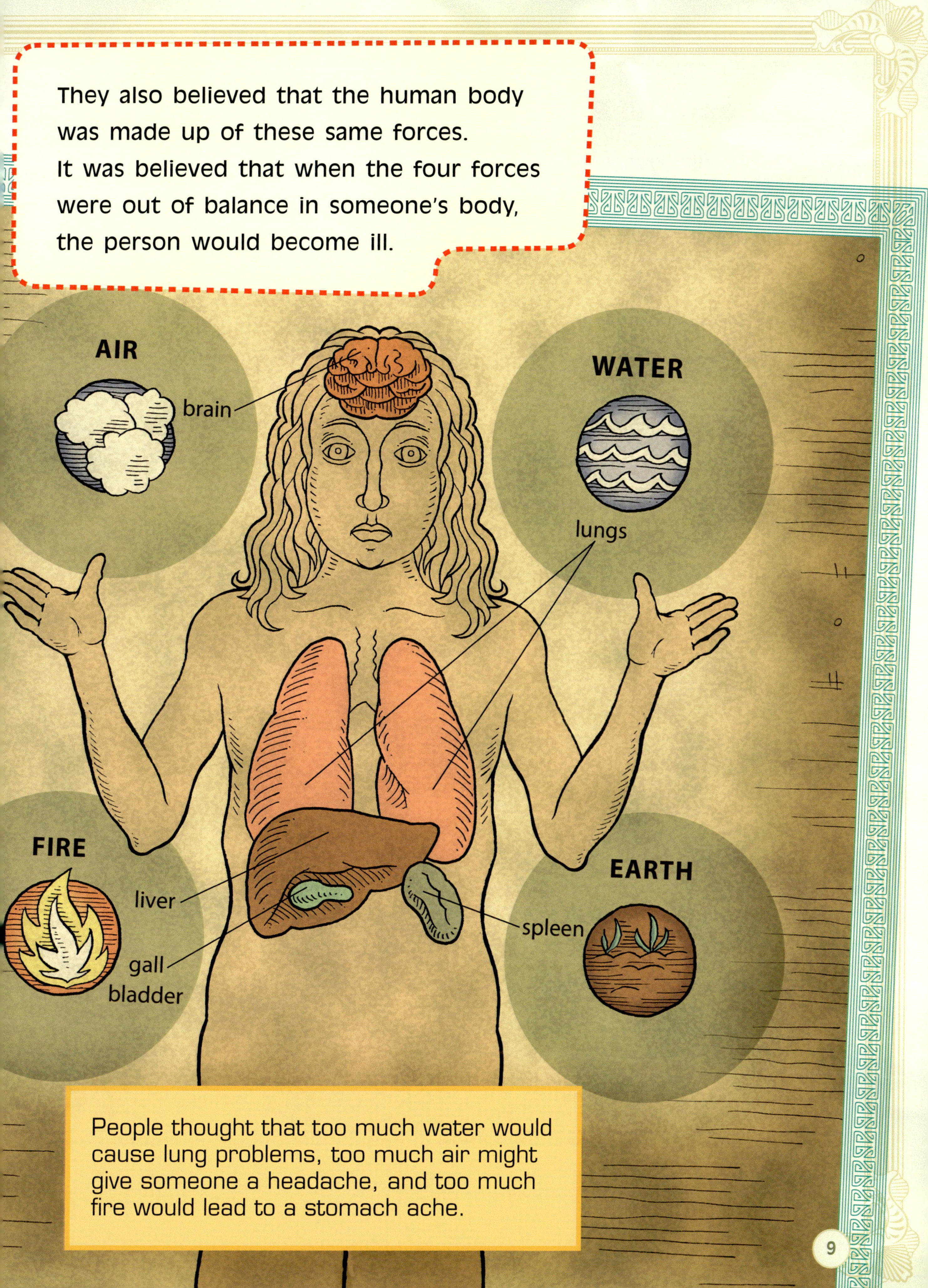

People thought that too much water would cause lung problems, too much air might give someone a headache, and too much fire would lead to a stomach ache.

God and the Planets

People also believed
in the power of God
and the power of the planets
over their lives.

When people became ill,
they sometimes thought that it was God trying
to punish them.
Others thought that the movement
of the stars and planets
affected their health in some way.

People looked at the movement of the planets and stars for direction in their lives.

astrology chart

CHAPTER 3

MEDICAL CARE

There were a number of things that people believed they could do to stay healthy.

These included living an honest life and being kind.
They also included eating the right foods and taking medicine.

If people became very ill, they would see a medical expert.
This could be either a person who knew about herbs or a doctor who used a wider range of medicines.

In the Middle Ages people would go to apothecaries to buy their medicine. Today, apothecaries are referred to as pharmacies or chemists.

Herbs

Herbs were the most common kind of medicine in the Middle Ages.
They were used by both common people and doctors for all kinds of illnesses.
However, sometimes a different kind of treatment was needed.

Sage was used to treat snakebites and intestinal worms.

Camomile flowers were used to relieve sleeplessness and headaches.

Cinnamon was used to treat colds and flu.

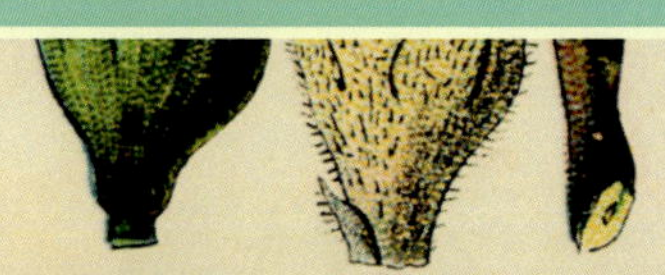

The flowers and leaves of some herbs
were made into tea for sick people to drink.
Many herbs were helpful for common problems
like colds, aches and pains.
They were also used on the skin
to treat cuts and wounds.

Blood-Letting

Doctors used **blood-letting** to help ill people. They did this because they thought that blood in different parts of the body affected the balance of forces in different organs.

There were two ways to let a person's blood.
One was to use worm-like animals
to suck blood from the person.
The other was for the doctor
to cut into different parts of the person's body
to draw off blood.

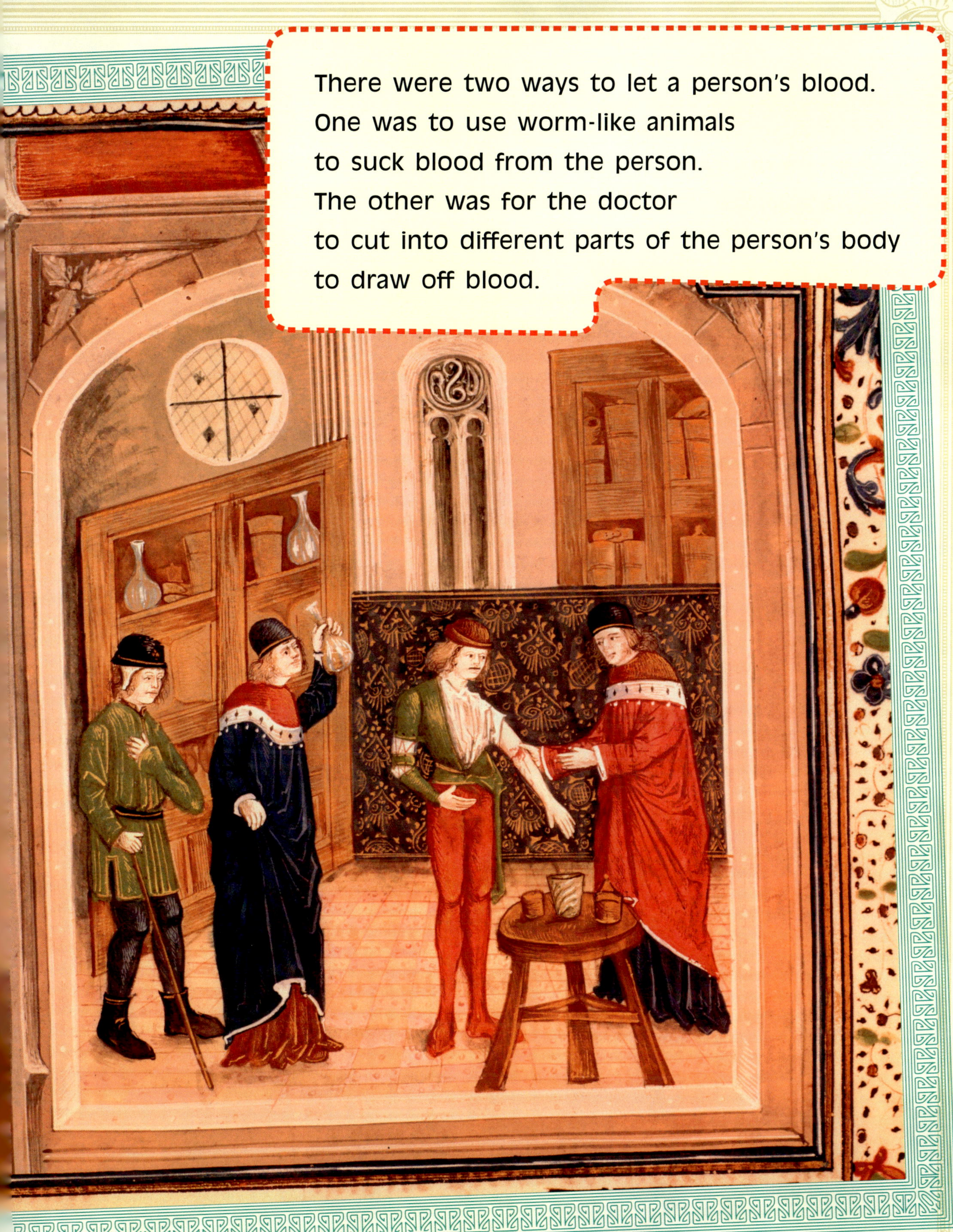

CHAPTER 4

KILL OR CURE?

The herbs given to people were not usually dangerous, but they were not strong enough to cure serious diseases.

However, other practices did more harm than good and many people died because of them.

Doctors sometimes used poisonous medicines, such as **mercury**, which caused many deaths.

Trepanation involved drilling a hole into a person's skull to release "bad spirits".

Blood-letting was very dangerous.
If too much blood was drawn from a person's body, they became too weak to fight a disease.

Bone-Setting and Operations

Sometimes people had injuries
that needed fixing,
such as broken bones.
So they went to a special doctor called a **bone-setter**.
The bone-setter knew how to put bones
back into place.

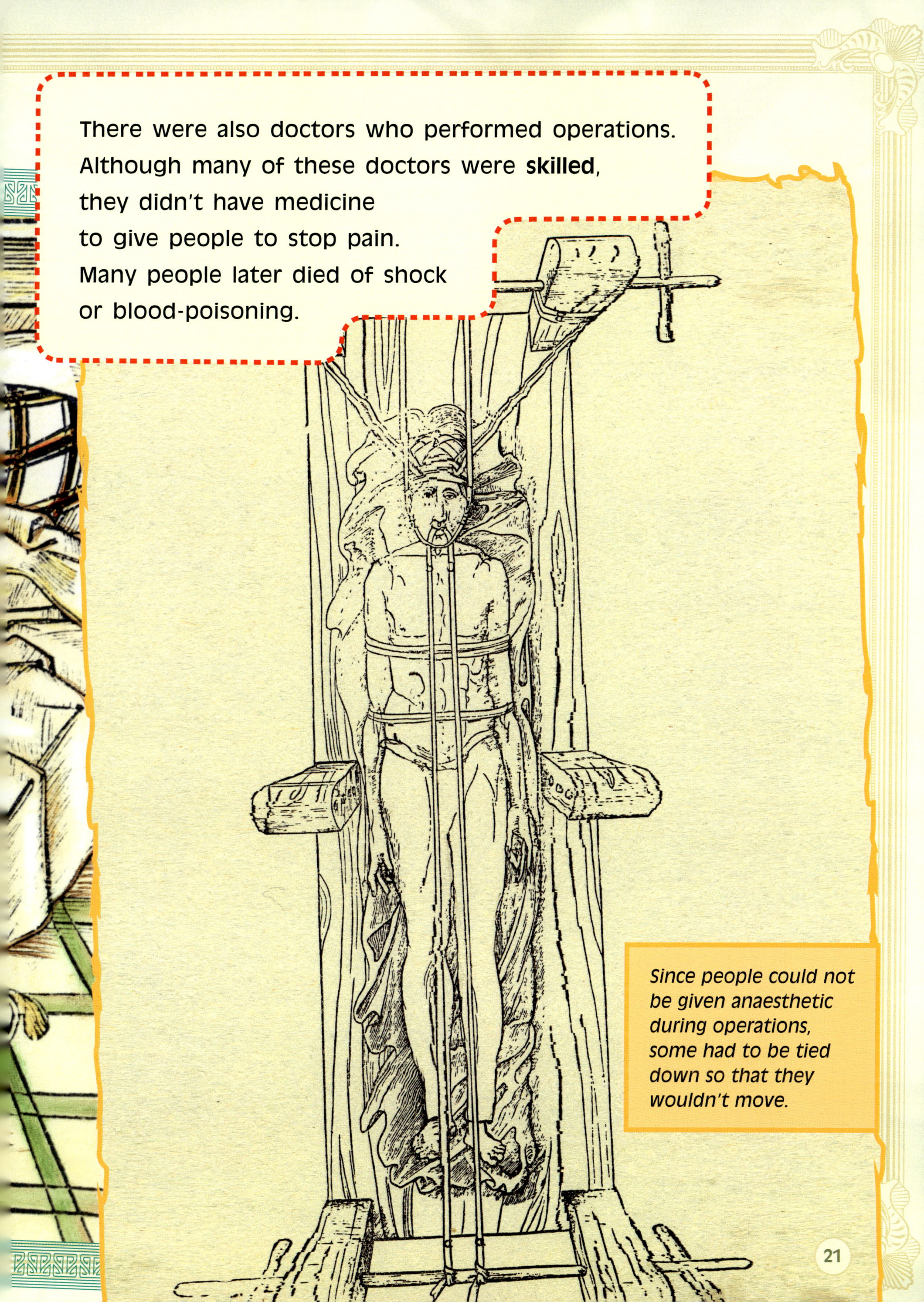

There were also doctors who performed operations. Although many of these doctors were **skilled**, they didn't have medicine to give people to stop pain. Many people later died of shock or blood-poisoning.

Since people could not be given anaesthetic during operations, some had to be tied down so that they wouldn't move.

CHAPTER 5

TURNING TO GOD

When people became sick, many turned to God for help. They believed that God had the power to make them better. People also thought that they would join God in heaven when they died.

Death was an ever-present part of life
in the Middle Ages.
People knew they always needed to be ready
to face death,
as it could come at any time.

Glossary

blood-letting a medical practice involving removing blood from a person's body by cutting their skin or using animals to suck the blood

bone-setter a person who set or put broken bones back into place

mercury a silver-white liquid metal

poisoning to affect with a harmful substance

skilled experienced or trained in an area of work or study

Index